31472400265181

D0432252

CARSON CITY LIBRARY
900 North Roop Street
Carson City, NV 89701
775-887-2244

WITHDRAWN

AUG 3 0 2016

With lots of love to Roger and Anne,
proud grandparents of Florence Grace
—C. F.

Ai miei nonni, al nonno Garibaldi e alla nonna
che profumava di vaniglia, alla nonna nell'ombra
e al nonno elegante. Con tanto amore
—J. A.

SIMON & SCHUSTER BOOKS FOR YOUNG READERS
An imprint of Simon & Schuster Children's Publishing Division
1230 Avenue of the Americas, New York, New York 10020
Text copyright © 2016 by Claire Freedman
Illustrations copyright © 2016 by Giuditta Gaviraghi
Originally published in Great Britain in 2016 by Simon & Schuster UK Ltd
Published by arrangement with Simon & Schuster UK Ltd
First US edition 2016
All rights reserved, including the right of reproduction in whole or in part in any form.
SIMON & SCHUSTER BOOKS FOR YOUNG READERS is a trademark of Simon & Schuster, Inc.
For information about special discounts for bulk purchases, please contact Simon & Schuster
Special Sales at 1-866-506-1949 or business@simonandschuster.com.
The Simon & Schuster Speakers Bureau can bring authors to your live event. For more information or to book an event,
contact the Simon & Schuster Speakers Bureau at 1-866-248-3049 or visit our website at www.simonspeakers.com.
Book design by Tom Daly
The text for this book was set in Artcraft URW.
Manufactured in China
0516 SUK
2 4 6 8 10 9 7 5 3 1
CIP data for this book is available from the Library of Congress.
ISBN 978-1-4814-7937-0
ISBN 978-1-4814-7938-7 (eBook)

My Grandparents Love Me

Claire Freedman

Illustrated by Judi Abbot

A Paula Wiseman Book
Simon & Schuster Books for Young Readers
New York London Toronto Sydney New Delhi

I'm off to Gran and Grandpa's
with a big smile on my face.

I always feel wrapped up in love
when I stay at their place!

Gran's big welcome hugs are warm.

Wheeee!

Grandpa swings me around!
He laughs—"You're getting heavy,"
as my feet fly off the ground.

My room at Gran and Grandpa's house
has special toys there too.

Gran smiles. "Have you looked on your bed?

You might find
something new!"

Gran's baking is delicious, yum!
And when I munch and chew
more cakes than Mom would let me eat,
Gran just smiles. "They're for you!"

Out at the funfair's splish-splash ride,

they don't mind getting wet.

Popcorn

I don't know how Gran's handbag,
which doesn't look that full,

has all we need
for our day out . . .

. . . it must be magical!

It's great to help in Grandpa's shed.
We build amazing things.

Gran hasn't seen our rocket—
ssshh!

It's red with silver wings.

I don't just stay at Gran and Grandpa's,
sometimes they visit me!

We all go out together then,
it's so much fun—
yippee!

Gran says I'll be a champion—
she's teaching me to swim.

With her beside me, I'm not scared.
Now I can jump right in!

Back home we all dress up and dance.
Gran puts loud music on,

while funny Grandpa jokes around,
and does the steps all wrong!

"Let's read this story, Gran!" I say.
We snuggle in a chair.

Gran's silly voices make me laugh—
pretending she's the bear!

Warm from my bath and tucked in bed,
I yawn. "I've had such fun!"
"Us too." They smile
and kiss night-night.
"**We love you, little one!**"